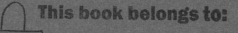
This book belongs to:

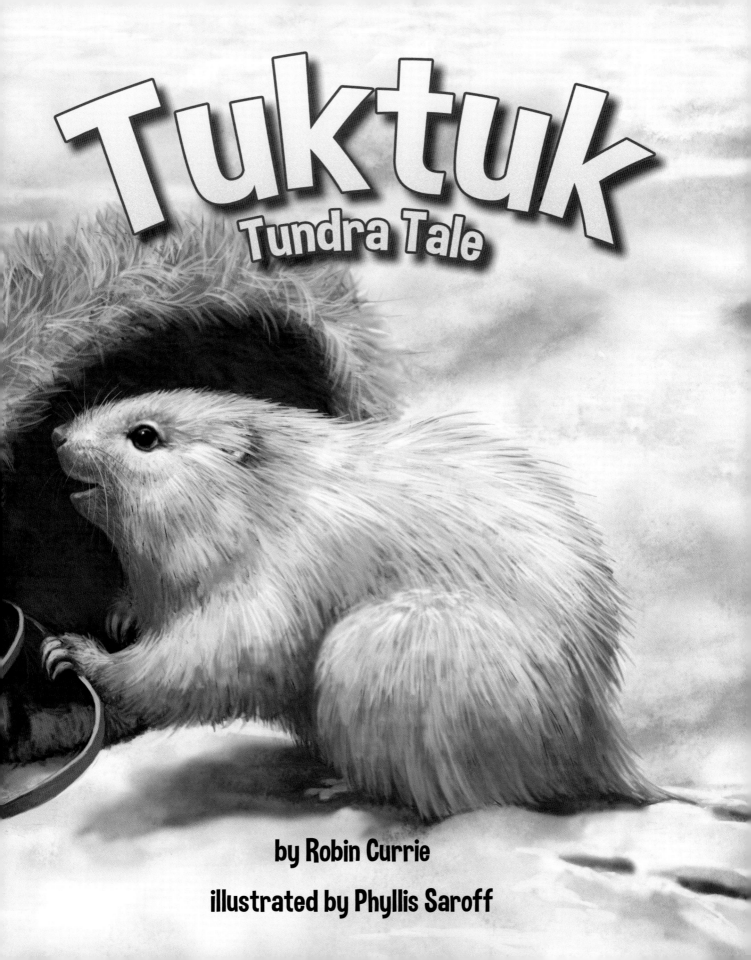

Tuktuk
Tundra Tale

by Robin Currie

illustrated by Phyllis Saroff

At the top of the world, an Inuit driver cried to the sled dogs. "Hike!"

"Bark! Bark! Bark! Bark!"

He saw the setting sun on the ice, but he did not see one furry kamik slip under the ropes and off the sled. "Hike!"

"Bark! Bark! Bark! Bark!"

Tuktuk saw what the driver did not.

Tuktuk hid until the dogs were out of sight.

The collard lemming was almost ready for the Arctic winter. His fur had changed from summer brown to snowy white. Then Tuktuk had used his long front claws to dig a deep hole in the hummock. Now Tuktuk searched the tundra for musk ox hair to line his winter nest.

"Perfect," he said. "One furry kamik
is just right for a collard lemming!"

As Tuktuk dragged it to his hummock, Putak the polar bear plodded out from a nearby pingo.

"Tuktuk," Putak called. "Winter is coming. Soon we will not see the sun at all. I need something to keep warm."

Putak looked at Tuktuk and said, "Ah-ha! One furry kamik!"

Tuktuk wanted that furry kamik. As the last rays of the setting arctic sun glittered in his little lemming eyes, he said, "Putak, you are right. You need this furry kamik. I think you should wear it on your . . . nose."

"Really?" said Putak. He pressed his face into the kamik until it stuck.

"Perfect," he said. "One furry kamik
is just right for a polar bear!"

Putak snorted. The musk ox fur inside the kamik tickled his nose. Putak gave a huge sneeze. *"Kerchoooo!"* The kamik blew right off and landed by Tuktuk.

"Humph," growled Putak as he ambled away. "No one needs one furry kamik!"

Tuktuk saw sun dogs glow on either side of the sun. He dragged his furry kamik toward the hummock, but Aput the arctic fox trotted by.

"Tuktuk," she called. "Winter is coming. Soon there will be no light for three long months. I need something to keep warm."

Aput looked at Tuktuk and said, "Ah-ha! One furry kamik!"

The glow of the arctic twilight sparkled in Tuktuk's little lemming eyes and he said, "Aput, you are right. You need this furry kamik. I think you should wear it on your . . . tail."

"Really?" said Aput. She twisted until her bushy tail was completely inside. "Perfect," she said. "One furry kamik is just right for an arctic fox!"

As she walked away, she swished her tail from side to side, and the kamik flew off her tail and high into the air.

Bash! It kicked her in the chin before landing in the snow right next to Tuktuk.

"Tosh," snarled Aput as she pranced
away. "No one needs one furry kamik!"

Tuktuk saw the first snowflakes and dragged his furry kamik faster. But before he reached his hummock, Masak the caribou tramped by.

"Tuktuk," she called. "Winter is coming. Soon all we will see is a whiteout that blurs the snow and sky. I need something to keep warm."

Masak looked at Tuktuk and
said, "Ah-ha! One furry kamik!"

Polaris appeared in the expanding night sky and glittered in Tuktuk's little lemming eyes. Tuktuk said, "Masak, you are right. You need this furry kamik. I think you should wear it on your . . . hoof."

"Really?" said Masak. She shoved a strong leg and hoof into the kamik.

"Perfect," she said. "One furry kamik is just right for a caribou!"

She stepped into the snow, but the kamik stuck in a frost boil. Masak pulled and pulled.

Splat! As it came unstuck, cold mud splattered the caribou. The kamik slid off her hoof and landed right on Tuktuk's hummock.

"Hrumph," snorted Masak as she galloped away. "No one needs one furry kamik!"

The Northern Lights shone in
Tuktuk's delighted little lemming
eyes. He dove in nose first.

Tuktuk snuggled down, curling in all four paws and every bit of his tail. He gave a happy sigh and said, "Perfect! One furry kamik is just right for a collard lemming!"

For Creative Minds

Polar Seasons

In the arctic winter, animals don't see the sun for six months. For almost three of those months, there is no sunlight at all. The rest of the time, the sun stays just below the horizon, giving them short, twilight days and long, dark nights.

In the summer, arctic animals have six months of sunlight with no darkness.

When winter comes, the animals have to be prepared for the months of darkness and cold. Some animals grow a thick winter coat, prepare a warm den, or even hibernate for the whole winter. But why doesn't the sun rise in the winter?

The Earth rotates on an axis that has a 23.4° tilt. When one hemisphere is tilted toward the Sun, it has longer days and more sunlight. At the same time, the other hemisphere has shorter days and less sunlight. The season in the northern half of the world is always the opposite of the season in the southern half.

The polar region in the northern hemisphere is called the Arctic. The polar region in the southern hemisphere is called the Antarctic. At the earth's poles, the sun stays low in the sky, even in the middle of summer. In the winter, the sun doesn't come up at all for months at a time.

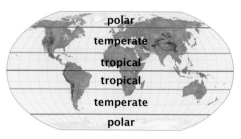

Arctic Skies

Match the following descriptions to the images.

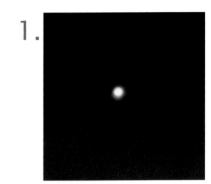
1.

In temperate and tropical regions, twilight happens every night when the sun goes down. But in polar regions, twilight can last for months. **Arctic twilight** happens in places north of the Arctic Circle. In the winter, the sun is just below the horizon. During the daytime, the sun never appears above the horizon, but there is dim light.

2.

The **northern lights**, or Aurora borealis, are colorful patterns of lights in the sky. They are usually green or pink, but can sometimes be red, yellow, blue, or violet as well. The lights are caused by tiny gas particles (molecules) in the earth's atmosphere. When charged particles from the sun reach the atmosphere, they collide with the gas molecules and create colorful patterns.

3.

Polaris, or the North Star, is visible from most of the northern hemisphere. The farther you are from the North Pole, the lower Polaris is in the sky. If you can find the constellation "The Big Dipper," follow an imaginary line from the two outermost stars in the dipper's bowl. That will point to the North Star.

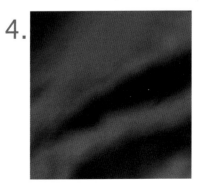
4.

Sun dogs are a type of halo. Tiny ice crystals in the atmosphere bend the sun's light. This makes two bright lights, or sun dogs, appear on either side of the real sun. They can be seen from anywhere in the world, not just in polar regions.

Answers: 1-Polaris. 2-sun dogs. 3-arctic twilight. 4-northern lights.

Arctic Vocabulary

Inuit Vocabulary

The Inuit are native peoples of Alaska, Canada, and Greenland. There are many different groups of Inuit people. The Inuit have lived in the Arctic for more than 4,000 years.

Aput: snow ground covering

Inuit: a native person in the Arctic region

Kamik: waterproof boot

Masak: wet, falling snow

Putak: crystalline snow that breaks into grains

Weather Vocabulary

Arctic twilight: the sun is not visible, but it is not completely dark

Arctic winter: no sunlight at the North Pole, from late September to mid-March

Northern lights: colored and moving reflections of the sun

Polaris: the North Star, directly overhead at the North Pole

Sun dogs: bright points on each side of the sun

Whiteout: sky and snow are the same color of white

Geologic Vocabulary

Frost boils: pools of partially-melted water over ice

Hummock: snow-covered ice mound

Pingo: mound of dirt and rocks

Tundra: ice desert with no trees

Life in the Cold: Animal Fun Facts

Collared lemmings are small rodents that live on the tundra of North America. They weigh only 4 ounces (112g), about the same as a smartphone. Collared lemmings grow up to 6.3 inches (16cm) long.

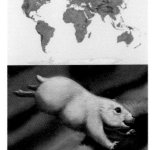

Collared lemmings have reddish-brown fur for most of the year, but they grow a white coat in the winter. This camouflage helps them hide from predators.

In the winter, collared lemmings dig burrows in the snow. Their burrows have tunnels that connect different rooms. Nests are lined with grass, feathers, and musk-ox wool to keep the baby lemmings cozy and warm.

Polar bears are the largest land carnivore (meat-eater) in the world. Polar bears grow up to 9 feet (2.7m) tall and 1300 pounds (560kg).

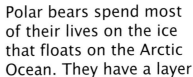
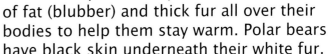

Polar bears spend most of their lives on the ice that floats on the Arctic Ocean. They have a layer of fat (blubber) and thick fur all over their bodies to help them stay warm. Polar bears have black skin underneath their white fur.

Polar bears eat seals and other animals for food. They look for holes in the ice where seals come up to breathe. Polar bears travel thousands of miles every year to find food.

Caribou, also called reindeer, live in groups called herds. They have large hooves that allow them to walk on top of the snow without breaking the icy surface. Caribou weigh up to 700 pounds (317kg). On average, they are 4 feet (1.2m) tall at the shoulder.

Both the females and the males have large antlers. Each year, the caribou drop their antlers and grow new ones in the spring.

Caribou eat lichen. Lichen might look like a plant, but it is not. Lichen is made of a fungus and an algae living together. In the northern hemisphere, lichen often grows on the north side of trees or rocks.

Arctic foxes have short, round bodies and thick, furry tails that are almost half as long as the fox's body. Their bodies grow to 26 inches (66cm) long, about the same size as a German shepherd. But they are very light; at less than 10 pounds (4.5kg),

arctic foxes weigh the same as a small terrier.

Arctic foxes curl up to sleep so that their tails cover their noses. This helps keep them warm in their cold, snowy habitat.

Arctic foxes use their sense of sound to hunt prey. They listen for small animals scurrying in burrows underneath the snow. They leap into the air and break through the icy snow as they land on top of their prey.

For Bob, partner in the greatest adventure—RC
For my special reading friend, Justice—PS
The author donates a portion of her royalties to the Chicago Zoological Society's Brookfield Zoo (www.brookfieldzoo.org).
Thanks to Julie Buehler, wildlife educator in Alaska, for verifying the accuracy of the information in this book.

Library of Congress Cataloging in Publication Control Number: 2016019118

9781628558791 English hardcover ISBN
9781628558807 English paperback ISBN
9781628558814 Spanish paperback ISBN
9781628558821 English eBook downloadable ISBN
9781628558838 Spanish eBook downloadable ISBN
Interactive, read-aloud eBook featuring selectable English (9781628558845) and Spanish (9781628558852) text and audio (web and iPad/tablet based) ISBN

Translated into Spanish: *Tuktuk: un cuento sobre la tundra*

Lexile® Level: AD 580L

Keywords: habitat (tundra), polar night, seasons, trickster

Animals in the book include collared lemming, polar bear, arctic fox, and caribou.

Bibliography

Dowson, Nick, and Patrick Benson. *North: The Amazing Story of Arctic Migration.* Somerville, Mass.: Candlewick, 2011. Print.
Labrecque, Ellen. *Arctic Tundra (Earths Last Frontiers).* Chicago: Raintree, 2014. Print.
Rivera, Raquel, and Jirina Marton. *Arctic Adventures: Tales from the Lives of Inuit Artists.* Toronto: Groundwood /House of Anansi, 2007. Print.
Silver, Donald M., and Patricia Wynne. *Arctic Tundra.* New York, N.Y.: W.H. Freeman, 1994. Print.
Sturm, Matthew. *Apun, the Arctic Snow.* Fairbanks, Alaska: U of Alaska, 2009. Print.
Taylor, Barbara, and Geoff Brightling. *Arctic & Antarctic.* Rev. ed. New York: DK Pub., 2012. Print.
Tocci, Salvatore. *Arctic Tundra: Life at the North Pole.* A Franklin Watts Library ed. New York: Franklin Watts, 2005. Print.
Yasuda, Anita, and Jennifer K. Keller. *Explore Native American Cultures!* White River Junction: Nomad, 2013. Print.

Text Copyright 2016 © by Robin Currie
Illustration Copyright 2016 © by Phyllis Saroff

The "For Creative Minds" educational section may be copied by the owner for personal use or by educators using copies in classroom settings.

Manufactured in China, May 2016
This product conforms to CPSIA 2008
First Printing

Arbordale Publishing
Mt. Pleasant, SC 29464
www.ArbordalePublishing.com